A BAYOU HOME

The Adventure of Swampmaster Bejeaux

Written and Illustrated

by

Nancy Backus

Fais Do-Do
Publishing

Fais Do-Do
Publishing

© 2015 Fais Do-Do Publishing

ISBN- 978-0-578-17393-1

Story and Illustrations by Nancy Backus
Copy Editor:
Graphic Design: Rebecca Livaudais
Printed by Garrity Solutions

Illustrations were done in pastel and ink.

2015 First Printing
Printed in the United States of America

For Riley, Felicity, and River

Alligators are the coolest creatures
And the very reptile my story features.

Swampmaster Bejeaux, as you will see,
Is a gator with lots of curiosity.

His home is in a Louisiana swamp,
A fitting place for him to romp.

A magical place with hanging moss,
cypress knees, and swamplands to cross.

You will meet his friends along the way
And several of them help save the day.

So settle in for a Cajun story
of Swampmaster Bejeaux in all his glory!

CONTENTS

A BAYOU HOME

The Adventure of Swampmaster Bejeaux

CHAPTER ONE
GOOD RIDDANCE

Swampmaster Bejeaux moved carefully, making sure to keep a safe distance from the trap. The Cajun hunters had cleverly hidden it among the cattails and water lilies that grew in abundance in the murky water of the swamp.

"I'z sick an' tired of doze rascals always tryin' to catch me an' skin me an' cook me in one of dem Cajun stews. Everyday it gits worse and worse. I'z gittin' too ol' to put up wit' dis aggravation."

Swampmaster Bejeaux let out a muffled roar to express his annoyance and crept slowly toward his den. He tried not to leave his telltale footprints in the soft mud and kept an eye out for intruders. He had just finished his lunch of delicious gar and was eagerly anticipating a long afternoon nap in the shade of his gator hole, burrowed in a mud bank by the edge of the swamp. Successfully arriving home, he began to adjust the Spanish moss in his mattress. Just as he was ready to crawl into his cozy bed, he heard a fluttering sound above the cluster of cypress trees that surrounded his home. The flying object maneuvered gracefully through the trees and landed on a cypress knee nearby.

"Swampmaster, Bejeaux, Swampmaster Bejeaux, are you at home? I have some important news to report."

This alarm was sounded by Arlene, a female brown pelican who had her nest in a tall water oak not far from Swampmaster Bejeaux's home.

"What's dis all 'bout?" Bejeaux answered, crawling out of his hole.

"I came as soon as I could, Swampmaster Bejeaux. You gotta lay low for a time. There's a whole gang of Cajuns around our swamp, and they're hunting for gators."

"I'z aware of dis, Arlene," Swampmaster Bejeaux replied. "I'z already seen one of doze traps, for true. I'z gonna keep a sharp lookout. An' iffen you see dem pesky rascals gittin' close to mah hole, I'da be much obliged iffen you would give me a sign by squawkin' real loud. I can move pretty fast iffen I don't have to move too far."

"Will do, Swampmaster," Arlene replied, puffing out her long tail feathers and feeling very important. She was a very friendly sort of pelican and took great pride in knowing everything that was going on in her neck of the swamp. "I think they should be leaving soon enough. I flew by their village this morning, and it looks like their womenfolk are fixing to have one of those fais do-dos tonight. They're cooking up big pots of jambalaya and andouille gumbo. I've also seen some other folks with instruments setting up to play some of that zydeco music."

"Oh no!" Swampmaster Bejeaux moaned. "Not another night of listenin' to dat racket. I can't seem to git no peace nowheres."

"Well, I declare, I couldn't agree more," added Arlene. "What's become of the good old days when we were left alone to the melody of the swamp frogs and crickets. Now we are constantly bombarded with the sound of shotguns and fiddles. It's a wonder I can get my darlings to bed at night."

"You knows, Arlene, I'z been thinkin'," Swampmaster Bejeaux confided. "I ain't gittin' any younger, an' I still gots some livin' to do. I'z startin' to feel hemmed in roun' heah. I can't go nowheres but somebody's tryin' to crimp my style and botherin' my peace of mind. I'z been thinkin' about goin' on a journey to fin' somewheres dat I can git me some peace an' quiet."

"Where have you been thinking about going, Bejeaux?" Arlene interrupted. "You've lived your whole life around these parts. All of your friends are here, and you are our leader. Mr. Bear on the other side of the swamp just made you godfather to his youngest. And the herons are always asking your advice about what fish are available in the swamp on any given day. And what about Hooter? You won't be able to listen to the latest news about the night activity around here, and . . . ."

"Yeah, yeah, I knows all dat," Bejeaux interrupted. "But I'z got de urge to strike out on mah own. Iffen I don't do it now, I'z never gonna do it. I'z gotten a wanderlust feelin' lately, for true. I can't rightly help mahself."

"But where will you go, Bejeaux?" Arlene repeated her question.

"Well, a while back I was talkin' to a heron passing through our swamp. He tol' me 'bout a real nice swamp a long ways up de bayou. He tol' me dat dere ain't no humans anywheres near dat spot an' dat it is very peaceful and quiet-like. I'z been thinkin' 'bout borrowing one of doze pirogues tied to some poles down on de bayou where de Cajuns live an' checkin' out dat swamp for mah own self."

"Have you lost your mind?" Arlene shrieked. "This swamp is your home. We need you here. Isn't there anything I can say to make you change your mind and stay?"

Swampmaster Bejeaux rolled his eyeballs around in his old scaly head and adjusted his long tail to make himself more comfortable. He seemed quite contented with himself.

"I may be crazy as you say, but I'z done made up mah mind. I'z gonna take mah afternoon nap now, Arlene. When I gits all rested, I'z gonna pack up a few things in mah knapsack an' head on out dis very evenin' when it gits dark. When I gits where I'z goin', I'll try to git word to all of you somehows. Now leave me be."

"Oh my," exclaimed Arlene, and she flew away to tend to her chicks.

CHAPTER TWO
A CLOSE CALL

Swampmaster Bejeaux had a long and restful slumber, dreaming of starting a new life somewhere else in the vast backwaters of South Louisiana where Indians and pirates had once roamed. He dreamt of sweet summer evenings with a warm breeze rustling through the Spanish moss that draped the live oak and cypress trees. He envisioned summer mornings with hummingbirds and dragonflies flitting through the golden haze hanging over the fragrant swamp azaleas. In his dream giant catfish leaped out of the water right into his waiting open jaws. Nowhere did he see Cajuns or hear their chatter or the sound of shotgun blasts. Paradise surrounded him.

Swampmaster Bejeaux awoke with these pleasant scenes still swimming in his head. The day had drifted away. Bejeaux stretched his stiff back and crept slowly out of his hole. The sun was now low in the late afternoon sky, casting

a rosy glow over the swamp. He quickly realized that he needed to hurry and pack for his journey. He grabbed a few pairs of tattered overalls (he wasn't much of a clothes alligator) and his favorite plaid blanket (being cold-blooded and all) in case the evenings turned chilly and he couldn't find a warm place to spend the night. Right before he started his journey, he gathered some small tree branches and some magnolia leaves to hide the entrance to his home.

By the time he had completed his tasks, the sun had set. The sky was the color of indigo, a deep purplish blue. A sliver of moon could be seen in the night sky. Wasting no more time, Swampmaster Bejeaux began to follow the narrow path that encircled the swamp. He soon came to another wider path that led to the Cajuns' small fishing village on Bayou Lafourche. He felt confident that he could secure a pirogue with some oars and slip away quietly without being seen.

At the point where the swamp turned to bayou, Swampmaster Bejeaux could see the Cajun village. Strings of lights had been draped from tree to tree and twinkled brightly against the night sky. As he approached, being careful to stay hidden from sight, he heard two children engaged in a serious conversation. A small girl with dark pigtails was seated on a low-hanging limb of an immense oak tree. A larger boy stood before her, hands on his hips in a defiant stance.

"I don't believe a word of it," the girl stated firmly. "Mamere must be making it all up so dat I will be a very good girl tonight and not wander off or git in trouble."

"I tell you it be true," insisted the boy who looked to be several years older. "I know it be true becuz I seen him mah own self."

"T Boy, you kidding, right? You seen de loup-garou, for true?"

"I sure has," T Boy announced proudly.

"So, what do he look like," the girl questioned, her eyes growing wide, "and how's it dat he didn't snatch you and carry you away?"

"Dat ol' loup-garou never got close to me. I couldn't see dat well in the dark, but it most sure had a hairy body and a head like a wolf with pointy ears and lots of sharp teeth. It was crouchin' in Pookie's hammock just over dere makin' growlin' noises." T Boy pointed to a group of swamp maples close to the bayou. "Its eyes glowed yeller, and I could tell it wanted to eat me real bad."

T Boy had never actually seen any such creature,

but he was taking delight in scaring his little sister. He
was a prankster and general troublemaker. But Mamere
had indeed told the children about a creature called the
loup-garou who lurked in the shadows at night and carried
away children who strayed away from their parents.

"When did you see him last?" the girl asked
quickly, hoping that it had been a long time ago.

"It was just last night, Janelle," T Boy said with
great authority in his voice. "I scared it away by yellin' dat
I was goin' to git Papa's shotgun and shoot it dead."

"Did you git Papa's gun for real?" Janelle was
getting very excited.

"Sure did! But when I got back to de bayou, dat old
loup-garou was nowheres to be found. He was a capon, for
true, and he must have skedaddled into de woods. Deep
down he ain't nothin' but a coward."

"I'z gonna tell Mamere right dis minute," Janelle
declared, and she sprang up and started running as fast as
her little legs would carry her, with her pigtails flapping up
and down.

"Well, dat ought to scare her real good," T Boy
chuckled aloud as she left, and he sauntered off, kicking
sticks and skipping merrily.

Swampmaster Bejeaux couldn't stop himself from

chuckling too.

"Doze Cajuns sure do like to make up tall tales," he said to himself. "They'z always exaggeratin' every little thing. Can't never seem to give a true account of what happens, no."

Bejeaux moved closer to the lighted area and saw that many food preparations had been made for the fais do-do. On one side of the opening there were several long tables with crisply starched tablecloths. On them were platters and bowls piled high with all sorts of Cajun dishes - seafood gumbo and steaming-hot rice, jambalaya, boudin balls, sliced watermelons, and ripe strawberries made into pies and ice-cream. Jugs of sweet tea and pots of hot cafe brulot were placed on a special table. The aromas drifted up Bejeaux's nostrils like a magic potion. He just couldn't seem to control himself. As if in a trance, he slithered right up to one of the long tables and crawled underneath the tablecloth. He started licking his chops and thinking about dinner.

Cajun menfolk started pouring out of the quaint wooden houses that were built high off the ground. Young mothers placed their babies in a special room in the hope that they would "go to sleep" (*fais do-do*) during the party. Some of the party-goers gathered on the porch to enjoy the soft breeze and moonlit ripples on the bayou. Others headed for the food tables. They piled their plates high and went to sit at smaller tables set up around the lighted area. The members of the Cajun band had placed their instruments on a raised platform. They soon started in with some hand-clapping, foot-stomping zydeco. The accordion player heaved his bellows in and out, the fiddler madly stroked his bow over the strings, and a third band member raked a spoon over a washboard. Dancers paired off and swung each other around the makeshift dance floor like well-trained acrobats. Even the children were joining in the fun. Some were playing horseshoes or bocce. Others were seated under a nearby tree with a deck of cards playing bataille, trying hard not to lose all their cards to the opponents. There was much laughter and talking and dancing.

Swampmaster Bejeaux was not the least bit interested in their merrymaking. It was all just a bunch of noise and nonsense in his view. But the food did interest him a great deal. His tummy was beginning to make gurgling sounds, and he had not packed any food in his knapsack. He was working up courage to grab a few seafood crepes when a bocce ball was thrown out of the field of play and rolled under the table, stopping right

next to Bejeaux. Before he could slap it out from under
the table, little Janelle lifted up the tablecloth to retrieve
it and saw a pair of yellow eyes staring back at her.

In an instant she let out a piercing scream.

"Help! Help! Mamere! Mamere! Loup-garou. It's
the loup-garou come to take me away! Mamere!"

Swampmaster Bejeaux didn't stick around to hear
any more of her cries. He took off with a huge lunge in
the direction of the bayou. He wasn't waiting for T Boy
to get his Papa's shotgun. He fairly flew through the dense
reeds at the edge of the bayou and plopped in the dark
water. With one swish of his powerful tail, he disappeared
under the murky water and didn't come up for air until he
had removed himself from harm's way.

When at last he surfaced, he could hear a big
commotion in the distance. Although no one but Janelle
had actually seen Bejeaux, the grown-ups did believe
that something had been hiding under the food table.
A knapsack with some overalls and a plaid blanket in it
was discovered. No one knew to whom it belonged and
everyone found this quite curious. Janelle was convinced
that it belonged to the loup-garou and T Boy did nothing
to dissuade her. The grown-ups were also befuddled.
Mamere stated that the owner certainly could have been

the loup-garou but said that the creature didn't normally carry a knapsack. Others thought the owner might have been a stranger passing through. Still others thought that someone was playing a prank.

But you and I, dear reader, know exactly who owned the knapsack. And Swampmaster Bejeaux realized that he had experienced a very close call. On the other side of the bayou, he was giving himself a good talking to.

"Ol' Bejeaux, you sure is a couyon. Yes, you is. You is a stupid fool. You is leaving home to git away from deze folks an' what doz you do? You git right smack in de middle of dere fais do-do an' 'bout git yourself kilt. Curiosity 'bout kilt the alligator this time, for true."

As Swampmaster Bejeaux continued to mumble to himself, he began to feel giant hunger pangs. But the fish had all holed up for the night. He was finally able to catch unawares a small snake and quickly swallowed it whole (which is what alligators do). Still hungry but mighty tired, Bejeaux decided to call it a day. He found a soft pile of leaves and crawled right in and fell sound asleep.

Back on the other side of the bayou, the commotion died down, the children were put to bed, and the Cajuns continued to "pass a good time" until the wee hours of the morning.

CHAPTER THREE
THIEVES IN THE NIGHT

Swampmaster Bejeaux awoke the next morning from a deep sleep. The swampland was aglow with a soft golden light from the morning sun. Bejeaux rubbed his eyes and looked around. He couldn't figure out where he was. Where was his cozy mattress? Where was Hooter who always arrived early to deliver the nightly news? He was disoriented and confused. He slowly stretched his aching muscles and vaguely recalled a fast getaway the night before.

"Oh yes," he finally remembered. "I was mistook for a loup-garou. An' for all dat, I didn't git to eat doze seafood crepes I had mah heart set on." Bejeaux looked around for his knapsack to change his overalls and realized it was gone too.

"I gots to pull mah own self together right soon," he said to himself. "I gots to git reorganized

an' make me a plan of action." Bejeaux sat quietly and
scratched his head with his sharp claws.

"I surely could use some help wit' directions.
An' I needs a pirogue. An' I needs mah breakfast," he
concluded.

Bejeaux sloshed out into the shallow water at
the edge of the bayou to wait for some juicy fish to swim
close to the surface. As he looked around for fish in the
morning haze, he spied a big log protruding from the still
water a short distance away. Perched on the log was a
rather large turtle sunning himself. He was a red-eared
turtle, a common creature in the swamps of Louisiana.
Lonely for his friends at home, Bejeaux struck up a
conversation with the turtle.

"How is de fish in deze parts?" he called to the
turtle.

"You talkin' to me?" the turtle replied in a slow
monotone voice. He clearly had been enjoying his
solitude.

"I is," answered Bejeaux. "An' since you obviously
live heah, I could use some assistance."

"And what kind of assistance would that be?" the
turtle slowly asked.

Swampmaster Bejeaux proceeded to introduce

himself and relate his journey to date. "An' now I needs a hearty meal an' a pirogue, an' I'll be on mah way."

The turtle didn't respond right away, and Swampmaster Bejeaux thought he had gone to sleep. "I says agin, mah friend, I'z in somewhat of a hurry. Can you help me or not?"

"Let me think . . . ," the turtle finally replied. "There are some rather big catfish to be found just 'round that bend in the bayou hiding in a big clump of irises. And since you don't seem to want to go back the way that you came, I suggest that you head north a ways. There are some Cajun fishing camps that way, and you'll have your pick of pirogues."

"I'z much obliged to you, Turtle," said Bejeaux.

"Tootles is my name," said the turtle. "And I was thinking while you were telling me about your itch to travel. I have been getting mighty bored around here lately. How about me coming with you on your journey for a while?"

"I don't mind one little bit," Bejeaux replied with delight. "I would be mos' glad for de company."

"In that case, you go along and get your breakfast while I pack up a few necessities. I need to say some goodbyes, and I'll meet you back here in a while."

"Dat sounds good," replied Bejeaux, and he swam away rather quickly since he now was terribly hungry. But his mood was greatly improving. So far, this day was shaping up to be a very good day. He soon found a plentiful supply of catfish and ate until he couldn't eat another bite. He took a leisurely bath in the clear fresh water away from the shore and then found a big live oak tree by the bank and sat under it to digest his meal and wait for Tootles to return.

The day was warm and sunny - not too warm for a late August day, but just right for alligators. There was a slight breeze drifting through the Spanish moss and the tall duckbill grasses at the edge of the bayou. Swampmaster Bejeaux could smell the sweet aroma of swamp magnolias. He roared a little to express his happiness and contentment.

After a short rest, Bejeaux made his way back to the turtle's log and found his new friend waiting.

"I've made my farewells," the turtle said, although he really didn't have much family to speak of. (Turtles are not known for their paternal instincts, you see.) He was traveling light, with only a small cloth bag of snack food, just in case he got hungry before dinner.

Swampmaster Bejeaux swam close to the

protruding log and suggested that Tootles climb onto his back until a pirogue could be confiscated. This arrangement suited the turtle, and he carefully mounted Bejeaux's scaly back and anchored his webbed feet.

The two swamp creatures traveled for several hours, meandering through a chain of bayous and swamps. They kept a sharp lookout for traps among the sedge and tall manna grass. They also kept a lookout for fishermen hidden among the tupelo and black gum trees that lined the swamp's edge. The day was perfect for enjoying the beauty of the swamp lilies, buttercups, and azaleas. Butterflies, dragonflies, and hummingbirds kept them company along the way.

"How much farther doz we got to go to git to deze fishin' camps?" Bejeaux asked.

"Not much farther," answered Tootles. "They are just around the next bend. But we need to wait until it gets dark. The Cajuns won't take kindly to someone taking their property."

"Mah short legs is already cramping since I ain't used to travelin' long distances," complained Bejeaux. "An' you is gittin' kinda heavy - no offense, mah friend. We could cover a lot mo' territory iffen we had ourselves a pirogue."

"That is certainly true," replied Tootles. "Maybe we can find an old pirogue that those Cajuns won't even miss. I've been up in these parts on several occasions, and I sure don't want to have anything to do with these fellows. They would cook me in a soup in a flash if they could catch me."

"I heah you, Tootles. Once we git a boat an' git on our way, I knows we can find de perfect home an' finally git some peace and quiet. We, I mean we gators, been heah long before deze humans come along. They'ze the ones done invaded our habitat. But look like we'ze the ones done got to keep moving out of dere way. It don't seem quite right to me, no! Did you know dat mah kind is known as living fossils?"

"That is most interesting, Swampmaster Bejeaux. But I was told by Mr. Toubs, the wisest turtle in these parts, that we turtles are older than lizards or snakes or alligators."

"Well, he be wrong, for true. Ain't no creature been 'round as long as us gators," Bejeaux insisted.

Swampmaster Bejeaux and Tootles continued to discuss this issue at length, with neither of them giving in to the other. (You might know the answer, but I don't.) After a long while, they both got hungry and decided to continue the conversation at another time and have an early supper.

Tootles made a salad out of the swamp plants in his bag, while Swampmaster Bejeaux went in search of some more fat catfish. The big red-orange sun slowly sank behind the cypress trees, and the rhythmic sounds of the crickets and swamp frogs signaled that evening had arrived. The two friends sat on the bank and discussed their plan of action. Since Tootles claimed to have exceptional night vision, the two decided that he would be in charge of locating a suitable pirogue to "borrow" and securing two paddles. Swampmaster Bejeaux would be in charge of watching for Cajuns and sounding an alarm if they were in danger.

Bejeaux and Tootles crawled back into the water and swam side by side as the bayou curved and entered into a small lake. In the twilight, several fishing camps were clearly visible dotting the shoreline. The structures were spaced about fifty feet apart, and each one had a small porch on the front side with a wooden walkway leading out into the water. The small cabins were constructed of cypress planks, and the roofs were made of sheets of tin. Each cabin had several pirogues tied to wooden posts situated by the water's edge.

While Tootles headed to one of the docks to inspect the pirogues, Bejeaux made his way to one of the cabins. The cabin was lit by candlelight, and Bejeaux crawled up to a window and peeked inside. He saw four Cajuns seated around a small square table in the middle of the room. Each man held playing cards in his hand and seemed intent on studying them closely.

Suddenly, one of the men who had a crop of red hair and a fat cigar in his mouth banged his fist down on the table and demanded, "Hebert, let me see doze cards you holdin' in yo' hand. An' don' you be tryin' to sneak a card outta yo' sleeve neither."

"You accusin' me of tryin' to cheat, Boudreaux?" another Cajun with a dark beard and bushy mustache yelled back.

"I declare, something sure is fishy goin' on 'round heah," Boudreaux replied. "You been winnin' dis heah poker game since we started. You beatin' all de odds, for true."

"Listen heah, Boudreaux. I can't hep it iffen I'z lucky," Hebert stated.

Hebert placed his cards face up on the table. The other players stared in amazement at the two aces and three tens.

"Full house, for true," Hebert announced proudly.

A mound of poker chips was collected by Hebert as the others grumbled in frustration.

"I'z gonna keep my eyes on you like a hawk, Hebert," Boudreaux growled.

The other men grunted in agreement and the game resumed. Swampmaster Bejeaux took his eyes off the men and looked around the room. On a long table close to the window was a big pot of gumbo and a platter of boiled crabs. A wire basket was filled with baguettes that looked to be freshly baked. The fragrant aroma drifted his way. Bejeaux's small brain immediately locked on devising a way to get some of that food.

Meanwhile, down by the water's edge, Tootles had chosen an old pirogue to confiscate that he hoped the men would not miss too much. He found paddles left in the boat which made it instantly ready for a fast getaway. Without wasting any time, Tootles slipped the rope from around the wooden pier. He was ready for Bejeaux to get in and take off. So . . . where was Bejeaux?

Tootles tried to make some noise that might attract Bejeaux, but his hissing and grunting couldn't be heard at a distance. Tootles stood on the dock contemplating how to get Bejeaux's attention. Looking around, a small object

in the pirogue caught his eye.

"What splendid luck," Tootles exclaimed. "A flashlight should do the trick." He climbed gingerly into the boat and reached for the flashlight underneath the seat. Pointing it in Bejeaux's direction, he flicked it on and off several times. Still, no Bejeaux.

Bejeaux was totally unaware of Tootle's signal. His eyes were glued to the feast awaiting him. He was determined that he was not to be denied a Cajun delicacy this time. He especially craved some of those boiled crabs.

The men had just finished another poker hand and one of them said, "It's time to take an outside smokin' break to clear mah head. I'ma gonna take mah pipe on de porch an' smoke for a spell."

"Dat's a good idea, Gisclair," the rest chimed in.

The old wooden chairs were thrown back in unison as the men rose from the table. When they headed for the front door, Bejeaux saw his chance. He grasped the windowsill with his razor-sharp claws and heaved his body through the open window.

The Cajuns headed in the opposite direction through the front door. As they stepped onto the porch, the light from Tootle's flashlight hit them squarely in the face.

"What's goin' on out dere?" Hebert yelled, looking for the source of the light.

"Why, someone's messin' with our pirogues," shouted Gisclair, and the four men took off down the steps, running toward the dock.

Tootles dropped the flashlight in the bottom of the pirogue and plopped over the side of the boat. He let himself sink in the black water, careful not to release any air bubbles.

Swampmaster Bejeaux had only gotten one mouthful of crabs when the racket began. He had forgotten all about his friend and the plan to take a pirogue in his haste to get to the food. Bejeaux lunged out the front door and down the steps. Seeing the men congregating by the lake, he veered to the right and made his way back down to the water a safe distance away. He could clearly hear the men's conversation.

"Mais, jamais d' la vie," exclaimed Boudreaux. "We done had ourselves a domion. But looks like we done scared that ol' peeping Tom away."

"No rascal better be tryin' to steal a pirogue, no," exclaimed Gisclair.

"Well, he be gone now," concluded Hebert.

Boudreaux grabbed the line on the freed pirogue and tied it to the post again. He then turned off the flashlight and put it in his pocket.

"You fellas ready to lose some mo' of yo' money?" Hebert said to the others.

"I'll see 'bout dat," answered Boudreaux. "Dis time, I'z gonna put a cunja on you. You won't be able to win a hand, no."

"We'll see 'bout dat," answered Hebert.

The men headed back to the cabin, smoking and laughing and joking about the unsuccessful thief. Hidden in some tall grass by the edge of the water, Bejeaux watched the men walk up the steps and disappear into the fishing camp. Soon enough, Tootles resurfaced. He spied Bejeaux and made his way over and crawled out of the water.

" Swampmaster Bejeaux, what's the matter with you?" Tootles asked. "Didn't you see me signaling for you to come? I about got myself made into soup meat."

"I'z most sorry, for true," the repentant Bejeaux replied. "I got mahself distracted up dere watching doze men jabbering away." (This was just an excuse, of course.)

"What do you want to do now? Should we give up on our idea to take that pirogue over there?"

"No indeed! We'z gonna wait till doze Cajuns call it a night and goes to deep sleep. Den we'z gonna slip in dat pirogue, quiet as wee mouses, an' be on our way," Bejeaux explained.

And that's exactly what they did.

CHAPTER FOUR
A STRANGE MAP

Swampmaster Bejeaux paddled for awhile without speaking to Tootles, content to watch moonlight filter through the branches of the cypress trees and cast eerie shadows on the surface of the water. Exhausted from the day's near calamity, his heavy head slowly fell forward onto his chest and his eyelids began to droop and eventually closed entirely. The oars slipped silently into the murky water, and the boat drifted along untended, carried by a slow current caused by a westerly breeze. Tootles had also fallen asleep, his head tucked safely inside his shell.

The two traveling companions remained asleep for the rest of the night. Swampmaster Bejeaux had a very pleasant dream. He was seated at a table upon which was placed a giant platter of all his favorite foods. As soon as he finished one platter, another was brought to him by Cajuns who seemed eager to please him. In his dream, the old alligator was not afraid of the humans. He was in charge and they were his servants. Tootles, on the other hand, dreamt of being caught by the Cajun fishermen who busily prepared to boil him in a big cauldron and serve him up as turtle soup.

As the first rays of sunlight hit the water, Swampmaster Bejeaux began to stir. His eyelids opened slightly. He discovered that the pirogue had drifted to the bank of the lake and the oars were gone. He stretched his old bones into an upright position. A strong musky odor hit his nostrils. Upon opening his eyes wide, he found himself staring at a family of muskrats standing at the water's edge. They had come to gather cattails for their breakfast.

"I say, are you lost?" the elder muskrat asked. "I haven't seen you around these parts."

"Mah friend an' I'z on a journey," replied Bejeaux. "I mus' confess dat I'z not at all sure where we'z at, or where we'z goin' for dat matter. I fell sound asleep, but we seems to have drifted las' night wit' de breeze."

Tootles had awakened to the sound of Bejeaux's voice and stuck out his head to see who he was talking to.

"Why don't you and your friend here join my family for a tasty breakfast of cattails. And afterwards, I might be able to shed some light on your location."

"Now dat would be mos' helpful," Bejeaux

answered, who was delighted at the prospect of breakfast. "But cattails ain't on mah list of breakfast foods."

"And I have my breakfast in my bag, right here," Tootles added, glad that he had hidden it under the bow of the pirogue. "But we could join you in a bit after we have our own breakfast. It would be very helpful to get our bearings before we continue on our journey. Where can we meet you?"

"Our feeding platform is not far from here," the muskrat pointed. "But we can meet right back here. I have a map that my grandpappy left to me that might be of some use to you. He told me it is a very important map and that I should take very good care of it."

"Dat sounds quite satisfactory to me," Bejeaux exclaimed, just as his stomach began to rumble with hunger pangs.

The little muskrats, with their beady eyes and paddle-like tails, followed after their parents to have breakfast.

Tootles took out his bag to retrieve his greens but found that they had wilted badly. He decided to eat some duckweed that was floating near the shore. Bejeaux went in search of a tasty gar to tide him over until lunchtime.

After a short while, the two travelers returned full

and ready to resume their adventure. Neither the muskrat nor any of his family were anywhere to be found.

"That muskrat must be having second thoughts," complained Tootles. "He probably figured you might eat him or one of his family members if you were hungry enough."

"Dat be true, mah friend," replied Bejeaux, "I admit dat I'z indeed eaten a few in mah lifetime."

Just as the two travelers were convincing themselves that they would have to proceed without help from the muskrat, here he came, waving a large parchment scroll in his paw.

"Here is the the map I was telling you about," the muskrat explained. "My grandpappy told me that this map was once owned by an old trapper who lived in a shack near here. He believed in voodoo and black magic. One day he disappeared and never returned. The rumor was that he was spirited away by a loa."

"What be a loa?" asked Bejeaux.

"I don't have any idea, but whatever it is, it must be very powerful."

"Well, let's have a look," Tootles suggested.

The muskrat untied the black ribbon that secured the scroll and carefully spread it open on the ground.

Bejeaux and Tootles leaned close.

"Hmmmm, dis is a very strange-looking map, indeed," said Bejeaux. He studied it closely. "I sees some bayous an' some trees, but I don't sees no landmarks dat I recognize. I knows dat I was born an' raised in de swamps near Bayou Lafourche. An' I knows dat Bayou Lafourche is de biggest bayou 'round heah. I don't sees nothin' dat looks like a bayou on dis map. Dis don't even looks like a regular map to me."

"I have never been able to make heads nor tails of it myself. But there is someone around here who can most surely shed some light on it if you are interested," suggested the muskrat.

"Indeed I'z willing to speak to him," said Bejeaux, who was always receptive to learning something new. "Can you takes us to see him now?"

"I can do that," replied the muskrat, "but I must tell you something first. This old creature is called the Wise One. But he is not at all friendly, and none of us should get too close to him. But you should be safe enough if you keep your distance. Do you still want to go?"

"What exactly is this creature?" inquired Tootles.

"I am just a simple turtle, and I am not a very brave one at that."

"The Wise One is a snake, an old cottonmouth snake to be exact," said the muskrat. "He lives on the lake's edge, not far from here."

"I'z not afraid of a little ol' poisonous snake," grunted Bejeaux, trying to muster some courage. "I will go talk wit' him alone iffen you will lead de way."

"I will show you to him," replied the muskrat. "I am anxious to finally understand this map, and I hope it will be of some help to you on your journey."

The muskrat started straightaway for the home of the Wise One. Bejeaux followed close behind, and Tootles lagged behind them both, not at all excited about the prospect of meeting a snake.

The snake's hole was a short distance around the lake, partially hidden by water irises and lilies. Upon arriving, the muskrat meekly called out, "Oh, Wise One, we are here to seek your knowledge." He proceeded to explain why he had come calling. A long silence followed. The muskrat and turtle began to fidget and secretly hoped that the snake was not at home. They slowly began to retreat and moved a safe distance away, hiding behind a large cypress tree and peering out from around its trunk. Bejeaux was left all alone.

Presently, out of his hole slithered the Wise One.

He was a very large snake, almost six feet in length. He was a grayish-brown color with dark-brown bands which encircled the length of his body. He was covered with keeled scales. The sliver of a pupil in green watery eyes darted in Bejeaux's direction. His forked tongue quivered.

"Let me sssseee thisssss map of yoursssss," the snake hissed.

Bejeaux was most assuredly frightened of this terrifying reptile. But he was determined to find out the secret of the map. With shaking hands he laid the map on the ground a short distance from the snake and backed away. The Wise One gyrated slowly around the map, raising his head and glaring intently at the words written on it. He seemed to be greatly amused. The snake opened its mouth and flicked his forked tongue.

"Very interesssting, very interesssting," he sputtered. "Where did you get thissss map?"

"Mr. Muskrat's grandpappy found it, an' he said dat it is very important. Do you knows what it all means? I'z on a journey to find a place to live dat is safe from hunters an' has plenty of fish, where I can spend mah ol' age in peace an' quiet. Do dis map show me where to find such a place?"

"Yessssssss," the snake replied, "and no."

"Dat is a very confusin' answer," interrupted Bejeaux. "Is it a 'yes' or a 'no'?"

"Be quiet, you impudent creature, and hear the wordsssss of the Wise One," snapped the snake.

"I apologize, for true," Bejeaux quickly added. "I just don't sees no familiar landmarks on dis map an' . . . ."

"I ssssaid to husssssssssh," spit the snake. "I will explain thisssss map in good time."

"But I'z in somewhat of a hurry, and I would likes to continue on mah journey."

"Life issssss a journey, you ignorant gator, and that issss what this map isss all about."

Swampmaster Bejeaux was now totally confused. He scratched his scaly head and hunched his shoulders. He stood quietly, wringing his hands, waiting for the snake to explain.

After a time the snake continued. "Thisss map shows the Nation of Loa. A loa isss a powerful sssspirit. He'ssss not exactly human becaussse he's invisssible. He isss a go-between the ssspirit world and the human world. There are many ssspirits that inhabit the Nation of Loa. Each one has itsss own ssspecial powers."

"Den I'z mighty glad I ain't in de Nation of Loa," said Bejeaux with a big sign of relief.

"Oh, but you are," replied the Wise One. "Every living creature resides within itssss bordersss. You can't essscape the powerss of the loa. No matter which path or crossroad you take, you will be sssssubjected to their magic. Thisss map sssshows three loa that accompany travelers on a journey. You would be wise not to upsssset Maitre Carrefour, the Loa of the Crosssssroads. Thisss loa can be a forcccce of bad luck for you and any traveling companions. And you might want to offer Grand Bois, the Wood Loa, sssssome leaves or honey to keep you sssssafe as you travel in the woodsssss. The third loa, Baron Cimetiere, will ssshow up when your life's journey comes to an end. You can't avoid meeting thisss loa. Sssome humans call thisss ssspirit the Grim Reaper. As for your destination on thisss part of your journey, I cannot tell you where that will be. It isss only for you to dissscover. Good luck to you and may you find what you are looking for."

And without further ado, the snake slithered back into his hole and left Swampmaster Bejeaux as bewildered as ever.

CHAPTER FIVE
A MONSTER STORM

As soon as the tail of the snake had disappeared from view, the muskrat and Tootles came out of hiding and joined Swampmaster Bejeaux.

"What did he say?" the muskrat inquired.

"Is the map helpful to us?" Tootles chimed in.

Swampmaster Bejeaux scratched his head and thought for a moment.

"De only thing I can figures out from what de Wise One tol' me is dat dere is lots of spirits floatin' 'round out dere watchin' our every move. An' iffen dey don't like what dey sees, dey gonna cause us a heap of trouble." Swampmaster Bejeaux continued to scratch his head. "I don't believes in no invisible spirits, no. I gots enough to worry mahself 'bout, steering clear of doze Cajuns dat I can sees plain enough. Doze humans is always makin' up some creature or 'nother, like dat ol' loup-garou dat de Cajuns conjured up to scare their littluns into behavin' and stayin' close to home. Lookie heah, Tootles, I aint askin' for much. All I wants is a satisfactory spot to live in peace an' quiet - wit' plenty of fish an' no humans 'round to pester me. As for de journey to finds dis place, it looks to me like I gots to travel down some bayous an' through some woods to git dere. But I don' plan to bother no loas along de way."

The muskrat carefully rolled up the map with his long claws and tied the ribbon around it. He tucked it securely under his furry arms.

"I plan to keep the map all the same. It may come in handy if I ever encounter a loa," concluded the muskrat. "Maybe it holds some kind of magic powers."

"You can believe in spirits an' black magic, iffen you wish. But I gots other things on mah mind. Did your grandpappy ever tell you 'bout a place in deze parts where Tootles an' I can live a peaceful life?"

"There are many swamps and bayous in these parts. I have never ventured far from my nest or family, but my grandpappy liked to travel some, and he heard a great many tales of faraway places. He told me about a grand river to the east that runs farther than one can travel in a lifetime. He said the river is very deep and the current is very strong, too strong to swim across. And he said there is a grand city on the far side of this river where there are many humans who don't want to see the likes of creatures like us, unless we are served up in a soup or used in making their shoes or coats. The name of the river, my grandpappy said, is the Mississippi and the city is called New Orleans."

"I'z glad to know 'bout deze places, so as to make sure I steers clear of dem," admitted Bejeaux. "We'z grateful for your help, but Tootles an' me must be on our way before de day is gone. I guess we be travelin' without a boat for a ways, since we'z lost our oars. Tootles, you can ride on mah back. You is too slow to travel on foot and keep up wit' me."

Tootles was glad of the offer. He retrieved his bag and climbed on top of Bejeaux's scaly back and tried to find a comfortable position. And so the two friends continued on their journey.

The sun was now high in the late summer sky. Swampmaster Bejeaux headed in a northerly direction, sometimes walking in a bottomland forest under a canopy of trees, including wild magnolias and live oaks decorated with Spanish moss, and sometimes swimming through a labyrinth of sinewy bayous and swamps, covered with watermint, yellow iris, and thick reeds and ferns. The bald cypress knees that grew upward from the roots of the trees dotted the murky water and created a scene of prehistoric times when dinosaurs and giant sea creatures inhabited the earth.

As the day wore on the temperature rose, and the air grew heavy and still. The two companions talked very little so as to make as much progress as they could. By late afternoon, Bejeaux began to feel strong hunger pangs. He arrived at a small lake and found a suitable spot to rest and eat a bite. Swampmaster Bejeaux suggested they go their separate ways for supper and meet again afterwards. He found some blue crabs nearby and ate them whole, shell and all. Tootles found some snails to satisfy his hunger.

The sun began to dip to the horizon, and the sky turned shades of lavender and pink. The water sparkled like thousands of golden coins. A great blue heron perched overhead in a cypress tree, silhouetted in black against the early evening sky. Spanish moss hung like greenish-gray icicles from the trees' spindly branches.

Swampmaster Bejeaux was filled with a "joie de vivre," a zest for life. He felt a profound happiness in his world of swamps and swamp creatures (not including humans).

"Why do I gots to share mah world wit' doze Cajuns?" Bejeaux asked himself. "I don't see as we'z compatible at all, no!"

While Swampmaster Bejeaux was contemplating his life, the heron above him began to chatter.

"Danger is coming. Danger is coming, I say," the heron cried out.

Bejeaux was startled from his thoughts and peered up at the bird.

"What danger is you squawkin' 'bout?" Bejeaux wanted to know.

"A very serious kind of danger," the bird continued. "And I feel it moving our way."

"What is movin' our way? Speak plainly so'z I can git out of harm's way."

"A monster storm with a mighty wind is coming. You best find a safe haven and plan to stay there for a while." With that warning, the elegant bird lifted his broad wings and gracefully flew away.

Bejeaux now took a long look around him and sniffed the air. Yes, the air was heavy with soaking humidity, and it was stifling hot. He noticed a flock of warblers swarming in the darkening sky as if they were trying to find a safe place to take refuge. It suddenly dawned on Bejeaux that he had not come across any Cajuns all day long. Maybe they were boarding up their homes and tying up their boats ahead of bad weather. In the fast dwindling light, Bejeaux saw low-lying clouds scurrying across the sky like an army of gray ghosts.

"I gits de feeling dat somethin' bad is comin', for true," Bejeaux muttered to himself.

Tootles soon reappeared, breathless and frightened. "Swampmaster Bejeaux, we've got to find someplace to protect us from wind and water. The fish have gone deep in the bayou, and I have seen some deer heading to higher ground. We need to move to higher ground too . . . and fast."

"I'z been keepin' away from de backroads dat I'z seen 'round deze parts," Swampmaster Bejeaux admitted, "but I guess we best head away from de low ground and git away from de danger of risin' water. We needs to find someplace to protect us from de wind too."

Swampmaster Bejeaux and Tootles started straightaway to find a suitable place to ride out the storm.

Now, you may be wondering what was happening with Swampmaster Bejeaux's old friends on Bayou Lafourche. Since birds live high in the air, they are very sensitive to changes in the atmosphere. Arlene had warned all the swamp creatures of the coming storm, and they had prepared for it as best they could. Then Arlene called a meeting of Swampmaster Bejeaux's old friends.

"I am worried for Swampmaster Bejeaux," she began, as they all gathered near Arlene's nest. "He can be very impulsive, as you all know, and I am worried that he has gotten himself into some kind of mischief. He may not realize a hurricane is coming and put himself in grave danger."

"Should we send a scout to look for him?" Hooter suggested.

"I think that would be a good plan. We will need a fast traveler though," Arlene added, "and a good tracker. It's no telling how far he has gone in the last several days. Do we have any volunteers?"

"Don't you think he can take care of himself?" grumbled Mr. Bear. "He's been around longer than most of us and has done just fine, for the most part."

"You're exactly right," a heron commented. "We have enough sense to stay close to home and not go chasing some fantastic dreamworld. He might learn a lesson or two if he gets himself into a bit of trouble."

"But we all miss him, I know. Don't you think we should at least try to find him and make sure he is alright?" Arlene pleaded her case.

"Well, I do miss the old gator," agreed Hooter. "And since I have very good night vision and can fly fast, I would be willing to try to find him and convince him to come home. I will try to reach him before the winds become too strong."

"That is certainly very generous of you," Mr. Bear had to admit.

"Yes, yes, very thoughtful indeed," the nutrias seconded.

"We all thank you, Hooter," Arlene concluded, "and we will be grateful to hear any word about our old friend. I hope you find him quickly and convince him to come back to us."

And so Hooter, a great horned owl with powerful yellow eyes, spread his broad wings and soared away into the menacing night sky to find his friend.

———◆———

While Hooter was beginning his search for

Swampmaster Bejeaux, Bejeaux and Tootles were searching for a safe place to take shelter. The night sky was blanketed now with the fast-moving clouds that hid the moon and covered the swamplands with a deep and penetrating darkness. The wind had gradually picked up and whistled through the branches of the cypress and oak trees. It started to rain, softly at first, and then harder and harder, slashing at Bejeaux's tough skin and Tootles's hard shell. The Spanish moss, which clung in huge clumps to the trees' branches, danced and swayed like witches' fingers. The frightened creatures came upon an old wooden shed and were able to enter through loose boards in the door but quickly decided it was so rickety that the wind would blow it away. They continued on to higher ground to avoid being caught in rising water. Presently, they saw a levee in the distance and plunged ahead as fast as they could travel.

When they reached the top of the levee, they realized that they had come to a road. They decided to take refuge on this high ground next to the road nestled against the roots of a giant live oak tree which had obviously weathered many storms.

"Stay low to de ground," shouted Bejeaux over the screeching and wailing of the wind. "Dis place is de best

we'z gonna find since de storm is reachin' full force."

Tootles had already found his spot in the curve of the tree's gnarled roots and away from the full fury of the howling wind. He tucked his head inside his shell as far as it would go. Bejeaux also used the tree to shield him from the wind and rain and hunkered down.

Time seemed to creep by as the storm raged on. The wind continued to bawl and howl. The rain fell in slanted sheets so thick and fast that Swampmaster Bejeaux could not see a foot in front of him. He had weathered hurricanes before, but this time was different. He was in a strange place with strange surroundings. He began to wish he had never left his home to go gallivanting around. He was far from home now and had lost his bearings. He was not at all sure he would find what he was looking for. In fact, he was having serious doubts whether such a place even existed. Cajuns had reached every nook and cranny of the swamps it seemed. And everywhere they went, they seemed to hunt his kind and many of his friends. Was there an alligator paradise out there? Or should he have been content with his home on Bayou Lafourche? Bejeaux had plenty of time to ponder these thoughts as he waited for the storm to pass.

The night hours slowly slipped away. When early

morning finally arrived, the wind suddenly died down and the rain slackened. Tootles poked his head out of his shell to look around. "Swampmaster Bejeaux," he called, "do you think the storm is over? Is it safe to move out from here? My spot is wet and uncomfortable, and I would like to dry out a little."

"We can git up on de road for a short while," answered Bejeaux. "But dis is jus' de eye of de storm, for true. De wind will pick up agin in a different direction an' de rain too. But we can take a look 'round now an' see how we stand."

Swampmaster Bejeaux and Tootles crawled up onto the road. From this high vantage point, Bejeaux could see that the wind had flattened the reeds and grasses and torn tree branches and thrown them like pickup sticks across the landscape. Some trees had even been uprooted and fallen over. Water had risen from the bayous and swamps, and Bejeaux was glad he and Tootles had moved to higher ground. The rising sun peeked through the scattered clouds and sparkled on the water-soaked land. He watched a family of raccoons scurrying across the road, looking for higher ground to wait out the back side of the storm.

"I hopes mah ol' friends is faring alright," Bejeaux

said to Tootles, "I clear forgot dat it be hurricane season in deze parts."

"Me too," admitted Tootles. "How much longer do you think this storm will last?"

"It be a big one, for true," answered Bejeaux. "An' it ain't over yet, no."

This was true enough. In a short while, thick clouds moved back in, and the wind and rain resumed. Swampmaster Bejeaux and Tootles settled themselves again by the live oak tree, and they turned their bodies to shield themselves from the wind which was blowing now fiercely from the west. Time marched on. The two swamp creatures were merely pawns in the maw of the storm. They tried to tuck themselves close to the old tree as the wind ripped the branches and Spanish moss from the tree and flung them through the air. Even birds who had lost their tight grip on well-chosen branches of massive trees were seen flying through the air at breakneck speeds. Mother Nature was displaying her power over the creatures of land and air.

After several more hours, the storm finally passed over them. Now that the roar of the wind and the pelting

of the drenching rain had subsided, there was a chilling silence. Not a sound could be heard.

"Swampmaster Bejeaux, is it safe to come out now?" Tootles meekly asked, pulling his neck far out of the shell and looking around. Seeing the alligator not far away, he repeated his question. "Can I come out now?"

Bejeaux didn't answer. Tootles hurried over to his companion. To his horror, Tootles saw the reason. A large limb that had been hanging above him had fallen from the massive tree and knocked Bejeaux out cold. Poor Tootles couldn't tell if Bejeaux was dead or alive. He continued calling his name, but Bejeaux couldn't hear him. Swampmaster Bejeaux was having a dream about fish flying through the air on a mighty breeze and barreling into his waiting jaws.

CHAPTER SIX
AN UNEXPECTED RIDE

Tootles was in a panic. "Bejeaux, Swampmaster Bejeaux, please wake up! PLEASE WAKE UP!"

Bejeaux, of course, couldn't hear his friend. Tootles continued to call his name. He pushed and tugged until he was able to remove the heavy branch from on top of Bejeaux's head. He tried to pry his friend's eyelids open, but they kept popping shut. He pulled his tail and pinched his nose, but Bejeaux remained unconscious. Finally, Tootles gave up and sat beside his friend and started to cry.

"What a fine mess we are in," he sobbed. "I don't know what to do. I don't know where to go for help." He looked around for any sign of life. "I don't even know where I am."

Tootles was exhausted. He had been awake all night weathering the storm, and now, here he was, in the middle of nowhere with his friend who was unconscious and possibly severely hurt. No one knew where they were, and no one would be coming to help them. All he could do was stay where he was and hope that his friend would wake up so they could move away from the side of the road. After sobbing in despair for a long time, Tootles finally fell fast asleep.

It wasn't long before Tootles was startled awake by the sound of an engine. The sound was faint at first but grew little by little. Tootles soon realized that something was coming down the dirt road in their direction. He knew this could not be a welcome sight, but he could not move his friend, and they were right beside the road in full view of any passersby. He frantically began pulling up some reeds by the side of the road in an attempt to camouflage his friend. The sound grew louder and louder until, suddenly, it stopped. Tootles looked up to find a Cajun staring out of the passenger window of an old pickup truck at them.

"Hey, Claude, I sees an ol' gator by de side of de road. Looks like he didn't make it through de storm. He ain't moving, no. He's a fresh kill, for true . . . an' good meat for a stew."

The driver leaned over and looked out the passenger window. "You is right dere, podna. An' his skin will make a fine pair of boots for de both of us. An' lookee dere. Looks like dat ol' gator has a friend. We can fix us up some alligator stew and turtle soup too. We best tie dat gator up tight, jus' in case he ain't totally dead."

The two Cajuns jumped out of their truck and went around to the back. Tootles tried to conceal himself behind the oak tree. He was thinking hard what he could do to save his friend and himself. But there was nothing he could do. The men returned with thick tape and a strong rope and proceeded to tape the alligator's mouth shut and tie the rope around his neck. They then got back in their truck and pulled it up alongside the alligator. With both of them bearing Bejeaux's heavy body, they heaved him up onto the flat bed of the truck. Swampmaster Bejeaux was still unconscious and didn't feel a thing. Tootles did his best to get away from the men, but being very slow by nature, they easily caught up to him and grabbed him by his shell. They lifted him up and flung him next to his friend.

"Well, it be good to have some good luck for a change. We is sure lucky to be alive after our camp washed away in dat hurricane, and we is lucky to find deze two critters to fix for dinner. Ain't dat true, Claude?" the man asked.

"You is exactly right," the other agreed. "We got to git to Bernadette's place. She still got her house cause she built it far away from de storm surge. She don't have no electricity, but we can cook deze critters up over an open fire and have a fine feast."

Tootles was able to hear this conversation and was shaking in his shell as the men climbed back into the truck and started off again. "Swampmaster Bejeaux, wake up, WAKE UP! We are gonna be dead meat if you don't WAKE UP!"

I don't know if the mention of food woke Bejeaux up, but he suddenly stirred and opened his eyes. Seeing Tootles right beside him, he started to speak. That's when he realized that he couldn't open his jaws. He took his claws and felt the tape wrapped tightly around his snout. He looked around and saw the ground underneath the truck whizzing by and heard the sound of the truck's engine as it moved fast along the bumpy road, splashing water up behind it. He looked imploringly at Tootles.

"I am so glad you are alive, Bejeaux," Tootles blurted out. "We are in deep, deep trouble. These Cajuns

plan to cook us for dinner. What are we going to do?
I don't want to end my life this way. Please think of
something and QUICK!"

Swampmaster Bejeaux shook his head to rattle his
small brain a little. He knew he needed to think straight
and fast. What to do? What to do? He started inching
his way to the edge of the flat bed and looked down. It
might kill him to jump out of the truck, but he had no
choice. He and Tootles would have to take their chances.
Bejeaux bobbed his head in the direction of the dirt road
to let Tootles know what he was planning to do. Without
waiting to talk himself out of it, he propelled his body
from the back of the truck. His thick body fell with a thud
on the dirt road. The dirt was soft and wet, and Bejeaux's
scales protected his body from the fall. He found that he
was is fine shape after his daring escape, and he looked
around for Tootles.

Tootles had tucked his head deep inside his shell
and jumped from the bed of the truck. His shell bounced
and rolled for a ways before it came to rest near Bejeaux.
He immediately stuck out his head and found his friend.
Joyous beyond words, the two companions fairly skittered
off the road and headed for cover under some thick
elephant's-ear plants.

Meanwhile, the Cajuns were gleefully planning their feast as they traveled along to their destination, unaware that their luck had suddenly changed yet again, and their supper had escaped.

CHAPTER SEVEN

HOOTER SAVES THE DAY

As I have stated earlier, Hooter had begun his search for the old alligator. Starting the journey at dusk did not present a problem for Hooter since he was a night hunter with exceptional vision in the dark. He was able to maneuver low among the trees because of his short wide wings and battle the fierce wind like a skilled aviator. The rain slid off his thick downy feathers. He swiveled his head effortlessly in all directions searching for his friend. He followed the path along the bayou, having been informed by Arlene that Bejeaux had started off in that direction.

Hooter covered a great distance in a short time, but he saw no evidence of Bejeaux. The wind continued to grow stronger, and the horizontal rain blew into his large eyes. From his vantage point in the air, it looked as if the land critters had all but disappeared. There was no one even to ask if they had seen the alligator. Soon Hooter decided that it was no longer safe to travel. He located an immense oak tree and took refuge in a deep hollow high up in its trunk to wait out the storm.

Just like all the other swamp creatures, Hooter had to wait a very long time for the storm to pass over him. As soon as the wind and rain slackened, Hooter ventured out. Water from the bayou had risen several feet, and where there had been land and lush vegetation, there was now only murky water. Many of the trees looked naked, stripped of their branches and leaves. The world around him was as quiet as the grave. The magical music of the swamp had stopped. There was no chirping or twilling of the crickets. The tree frogs were not croaking. The song of chuck-will's-widow was not playing this day. Hooter did not feel like hooting.

But Hooter had made a commitment to find Swampmaster Bejeaux. He rallied and began his search once again. He flew to higher ground, knowing that Bejeaux would have moved there too. He began to see some signs of life. He found a family of raccoons who were trying to return to their soggy home.

"Have you seen an old alligator with blue overalls and a red-checked bandanna?" he inquired.

"We have seen many alligators passing this way," they replied, "but none of them match your description."

Hooter asked some pelicans high up in a cypress

tree. They had not seen Bejeaux. He next asked a group of deer who were hungrily eating acorns that had fallen from a live oak tree. They had not seen Bejeaux either. Hooter had spent the better part of the day in his pursuit when he finally came across the family of muskrats that Bejeaux had encountered the previous day. They were glad to point Hooter in the right direction and informed him that the alligator was traveling with a large turtle.

Hooter was greatly cheered and encouraged by this news. He soared high up in the late afternoon sky. The clouds were gone, and the sun was bright. He was able to see a great distance and flew effortlessly and gracefully, peering below for any sign of Swampmaster Bejeaux and the turtle. And soon enough, Hooter spied the two creatures, partially hidden among the clump of elephant's-ear plants.

Swampmaster Bejeaux and Tootles had slowly gathered their wits. Tootles used his sharp beak to loosen the tape around Bejeaux's snout. Swampmaster Bejeaux used his claws to remove the rope from around his neck. They were assessing their situation when Hooter landed in a wild magnolia tree nearby.

"Swampmaster Bejeaux, my friend, I am surely glad to see that you are alive," Hooter began. "Your friends sent me to find you and convince you to come back to your home."

"An' I'z most glad to see you too, Hooter. I'z glad to be alive, for true. Dis heah is Tootles, mah new friend, and we'z had several close calls. I'z just now calm enough to talk 'bout it."

Swampmaster Bejeaux told Hooter about his recent adventures - his fast getaway at the fais do-do, the snatching of the pirogue from the fishing camp, and his lucky escape from the hungry Cajuns.

"You knows, Hooter, I left mah home to find some peace an' quiet. But all I'z been findin' is a heap of trouble. De more I try to git away from humans, de more I seem to run smack dab into dem. I ain't been havin' a good time at all, no. I'z been runnin' for mah life mos' of de time an' been knocked out along de way. I should have stayed at home where I belongs. You come jus' at de right time. I'z lost mah way, for true, an' I hopes you can lead me home. I'z mos' grateful to you an' mah friends for tryin' to find me. I sure is lucky to have good friends dat care 'bout ol' Bejeaux."

"I hope you have learned your lesson, Swampmaster Bejeaux. I've flown all over these parts, and I think you should be content with your old swamp.

You're good at avoiding those traps, and besides, you have been our swamp master for many years."

"I don't rightly know what got into me, no. I'z been missing all of mah good friends back dere." Swampmaster Bejeaux was truly sorry that he had taken his friends for granted.

"I suggest we rest here today and start our journey home in the morning," Hooter said. "Hopefully, by then the water will have gone down some, and you can make your way on dry land."

"I would agree wit' dat," added Swampmaster Bejeaux. "Mah poor ol' body needs a rest, for true. I'z got a mighty bump on mah head, and I'z sore all over. Hopefully by mornin', I'll be feelin' better. I'z looking forward to goin' home, an' dat's a fact."

The three companions chatted until nightfall, glad to see the beautiful sunset again and the water starting to recede. Bejeaux had a giant appetite and left his friends to forage for something to eat. He had to settle for some small birds and fish that hadn't survived the storm. Tootles settled for some swamp grasses that had been uprooted. Hooter decided to wait until later to hunt for his dinner.

Swampmaster Bejeaux and Tootles found a

comfortable spot hidden among some bull-tongue plants. Hooter flew away to satisfy his hunger and find a suitable tree branch to spend the rest of the night. It had been a trying several days for the swamp creatures. As Swampmaster Bejeaux was falling asleep, he gave a heartfelt bellow of satisfaction. He felt happy inside. He was going home.

CHAPTER EIGHT
THE REVELATION

As soon as the sun was up and the three companions had searched for a meager breakfast, they began their journey home. It was a sad sight that met their eyes that day. The ground was littered with jagged tree branches and flattened vegetation, and it was hard staying on a straight path for very long. Deep pools of water from the lakes and bayous still covered much of the bottomland, and the travelers had to weave in and out of soggy debris. Hooter knew the way back, which was quite lucky because Swampmaster Bejeaux and Tootles had lost their bearing entirely in the destruction left by the storm.

The burrows and nests of the swamp creatures had either been flooded or blown away in the storm, and creatures of all kinds had lost their homes and food supplies. Swampmaster Bejeaux knew that his neck of the swamp would not have been spared either. He shuttered to think what his old home would look like when he returned.

As the three travelers passed along the lake that

had been dotted with the fishing camps, they saw that
the Cajuns had not escaped the power of Mother Nature
either. The wooden structures had been blown away or
swept off their wooden piers. They had broken apart or
were lying at strange angles on the land. Human valuables
had been flung far and wide. Bejeaux spotted a chair
perched in an uprooted tree and some broken dishes and
glassware scattered nearby. He even found some of the
Cajuns' playing cards in a clump of cattails. It was as if
nature had decided to play a trick on all the inhabitants of
the swamplands and rearrange the landscape - destroying
or moving everything in her grasp.

The morning passed slowly as Swampmaster Bejeaux and Tootles trudged along on the ground, and Hooter served as navigator from the air. They finally stopped around noon to rest for a while.

"You knows, Hooter and Tootles," Bejeaux began as they were resting. "dis journey has caused me to rearrange mah thinkin', jus' like de hurricane has rearranged de swamp 'round heah. I seems to see mah situation in a much clearer light. I ain't so keen to go off lookin' for de perfect place to live out mah ol' age. I thinks now dat I gots to try an' make wherever I is de perfect place to be. I don't needs no loup-garou to scare me into stayin' put no more. An' I sure don't needs to aggravate no loas to cause me any mo' trouble. I even sees doze pesky Cajuns in a different way. De gots dere problems too, jus' like we does."

"That all sounds quite reasonable and straight-thinking, Swampmaster Bejeaux," replied Tootles. "I think I might like to stay with you for a while longer to meet your good friends that care for you so much."

"You'z mos' welcome to do so. I thinks you will find dem all very agreeable indeed," added Bejeaux, "an' I knows dere's gonna be loads of work to be done when I gits home. An' I'z good at supervisin', for true. After all,

I'z the Swampmaster."

After their brief rest, the threesome continued on. The sun was bright in the late August sky, and the heat and scattered debris drove the water-loving creatures back into the bayou where they drifted slowly along. Hooter glided over them, guiding them in the right direction. Toward late afternoon, Bejeaux began to recognize some old landmarks. He came across a watering hole that was a favorite place to find catfish. The fish had returned close to the surface of the water, and Bejeaux had a sumptuous dinner. Many of the swamp plants had lifted themselves toward the sun again after being blown down or covered with water. Tootles was delighted to find some water hyacinth and alligator weed. Hooter located a still-standing cypress tree and took a nap in the shade of its branches.

Satisfied after a refreshing break in their travels, the companions sat on a fallen tree branch and watched the half-moon rise over the wetlands. Stars appeared in the night sky and twinkled like Christmas lights above the cypress forest. The warm-muck aroma of the swampland was pleasant and comforting to Bejeaux. The music of the swamp could be heard again - the chirps and twills of crickets, the croaks and squeaks of tree frogs, the

call of the whippoorwills, and the screech of the owls. The
world of Swampmaster Bejeaux was beginning to come
alive again. He was very glad to be a part of it.

"We'z been through a bad spell, for true,"
Swampmaster Bejeaux commented to his friends. "I guess
I mus' have aggravated one of doze wood loas dat ol' snake
was speakin' 'bout. Maybe dey really do exist. I'z even
startin' to believe in dat ol' loup-garou dat little boy say
he saw. I'z been seein' some yeller eyes dartin' through de
branches of deze heah cypress trees from time to time. I'z
gonna be glad to gits back to mah ol' den an' mah cozy
mattress."

"I'm afraid your home may be all soggy and rearranged by the hurricane," Tootles replied. "Your friends may have to rebuild their homes too."

"Dat may be true, Tootles," Swampmaster Bejeaux agreed. "An' I'z ready to do mah part to make sure everythin' is put back in its proper place an' better den ever."

"I'm going to get a good night's sleep," Tootles said, "so we can be sure to have the energy to make it home tomorrow without fail."

"You'z a very sensible turtle, Tootles. I'z glad dat we met, for true."

Swampmaster Bejeaux and Tootles found a comfortable spot under a mat of swamp grasses and settled in for the night, while Hooter began his hunt for some crabs and crawfish to eat for dinner.

CHAPTER NINE
A TRAP

The following morning dawned bright and promising. Swampmaster Bejeaux and Tootles ate a hearty breakfast, Hooter carefully preened his feathers with his talons, and then the group embarked on the last leg of their journey home.

The weary travelers were now in familiar territory and they quickened their pace, anxious to get back home. They were each deep in thought as they continued to maneuver through the debris left behind from the hurricane.

Suddenly, the comforting sounds of the swamp were interrupted by a loud SNAP. Swampmaster Bejeaux felt a searing pain in his back leg. He swung his heavy head around and saw a terrible sight. His leg was caught in a hunter's trap. He instinctively tried to pull and twist his leg out of the razor-sharp clutches of the trip-snare trap but with no success. His worst nightmare had finally come true. He was trapped.

"I'z caught in dat ol' Cajun trap, for true,"

Swampmaster Bejeaux bellowed in pain. "I can't seems to git loose. I'z a goner, for true. An' I was almos' home - back to mah ol' friends and sof' mattress. Dis is a cruel, cruel happenin' - mos' cruel. What did I do to deserve dis? Doze loas has done me in, I 'spect."

"Don't give up now, Swampmaster Bejeaux," Tootles pleaded. He looked at Hooter for help. "What can we do to save him, Hooter? There must be something we can do."

Tootles tried to pull the teeth of the trap open with his beak with no success. He could see the gash in the alligator's leg and started to sob in anguish and despair.

Hooter surveyed the surrounding bottomland for humankind but could see no sign of hunters. "This trap has likely washed here from someplace else. At least we might have some time to stage a rescue. I will fly home and bring Mr. Bear back with me. He is the only one who is strong enough to open this trap. And Arlene can bring supplies to bind your leg so you can hopefully make it back home. Tootles, try to hide Swampmaster with leaves so no hunter will see him. And stop your sobbing and try to comfort our unfortunate friend," he concluded, as Tootles seemed to be making matters worse.

Hooter immediately soared away, darting through

the sunlit haze like a well-aimed arrow and soon disappearing. Tootles quickly started gathering leaves and twigs to cover Swampmaster Bejeaux, who lay still, moaning in pain.

"Dis be a sad endin' to ol' Bejeaux," Swampmaster Bejeaux said mostly to himself. "Mah spirits was so high, and I had such grand plans for mah future. But . . . look at me now . . . oh, mah leg hurts, for true."

"Please don't lose hope, Swampmaster Bejeaux. Hooter can fly fast, and your good friends will come to your rescue, I'm sure," Tootles spoke with encouragement.

And so passed the morning with Swampmaster Bejeaux moaning and groaning and Tootles gathering leaves and speaking words of encouragement.

———◆———

Hooter arrived home at noontime. He quickly rounded up the swamp creatures and delivered the bad news about Swampmaster Bejeaux. He wasted no time in explaining his rescue plan.

Arlene, in her usual efficient manner, set about getting the needed supplies to tend to Swampmaster Bejeaux's wound, and Mr. Bear postponed looking for a new house, necessitated by the hurricane. In no time, the rescue team started off, with Hooter leading the way. Mr. Bear lumbered as fast as he could to keep up with Arlene and Hooter, while keeping to familiar paths that were relatively passable. Arlene grew weary of carrying her first aid supplies and asked Hooter to carry them in his strong talons.

They arrived at their destination in mid-afternoon. They found Tootles huddled close to Swampmaster Bejeaux who was still alive but much subdued. He barely noticed that his good friends had arrived.

Mr. Bear brushed the leaves from Swampmaster Bejeaux and surveyed the trap. "I will try to open the trap if you will move Swampmaster Bejeaux's leg from its clutches," he spoke to the turtle.

"I will gladly do it," agreed Tootles. "He is barely conscious, I fear."

"Hang on, my old friend," Mr. Bear spoke softly to Swampmaster Bejeaux. "I am going to try to free your leg. Your friends back on the bayou are anxious to have you home."

Swampmaster Bejeaux opened his eyes and tried to reply but could only manage to moan a little. Mr. Bear put all his strength into saving Swampmaster Bejeaux. With a rusty creak, the trap was pried open and Tootles pulled

Swampmaster Bejeaux's leg free. Swampmaster Bejeaux emitted a weak sigh of relief.

Arlene now took command and gently washed the alligator's wound with cool, fresh water. She masterfully plastered his leg with a mixture of wet Spanish moss and bird feathers and fashioned a cast that would protect Swampmaster Bejeaux's leg as he moved. Hooter gathered some catfish and fed them to Swampmaster Bejeaux to give him

strength to make the trip home.

The group kept watch over Swampmaster Bejeaux while his cast dried, and they waited for him to rally enough to travel. Swampmaster Bejeaux's spirits slowly but surely began to lift again. His leg had stopped throbbing, and he realized he had escaped a tragic end once again. He was extremely happy to see Arlene and Mr. Bear and was anxious to get safely home as quickly as possible.

"Iffen you would be patient wit' your ol' friend, I would like to try to git home now," Swampmaster Bejeaux finally stated. "It would be so fine to be home befo' de day is done."

With the guidance and encouragement of his friends, Swampmaster Bejeaux ever so slowly covered the distance back to Bayou Lefourche.

CHAPTER TEN
THE CELEBRATION

Swampmaster Bejeaux's bayou home was bathed in moonlight when he and his friends arrived. Most of its inhabitants had gone to bed. He humbly and sincerely thanked Arlene and Mr. Bear for coming to his aid. He was completely exhausted, and his leg was throbbing again with a dull pain. When he was told that his home had washed away, he and Tootles simply found an old fallen cypress tree and crawled under part of the trunk. Although Swampmaster Bejeaux was without his burrow and familiar belongings, he

was happy and content in knowing that he was home at last. He quickly fell into a sound and peaceful sleep that lasted the rest of the night and the entirety of the next day.

On the other hand, as soon as the

sun began to rise in the sky, Arlene was up and busy organizing a proper "welcome home" celebration for Swampmaster Bejeaux and his loyal friend, Tootles. She rounded up as many of the swamp's inhabitants as she could find.

"We simply must clear a big space and arrange a place for all of Swampmaster Bejeaux's friends to sit and hear about his adventure," Arlene said to Mr. Bear and Mrs. Raccoon.

"I will move these tree branches and find a nice large log for Swampmaster Bejeaux to sit on and rest his leg," Mr. Bear offered.

"I will go and prepare a special pie of juicy catfish and speckled trout, and for dessert I'll make an elderberry and pecan cobbler," Mrs. Raccoon said proudly. "I know how Swampmaster Bejeaux loves my cooking, and I was able to store a few things that survived the storm."

"And I will fly far and wide and personally invite all of his friends and their little ones. We will want everyone here to listen to what experiences he had on his travels," Hooter added.

"Excellent, excellent!" exclaimed Arlene. "We will let Swampmaster Bejeaux and his friend, Tootles, rest today. That will give us plenty of time to prepare for the celebration tomorrow."

The swamp animals spent the day repairing their damaged homes and making preparations for the swamp creatures' fais do-do. Arlene's nest had blown away.

Arlene's mate picked out a new site, and Arlene busily gathered reeds and grasses and sticks to replace her old nest. The nutria family's den was filled with water, so they dug a new burrow on higher ground and gathered swamp grasses to line the den within. The muskrat family also had to build a new lodge out of aquatic plants and picked choice cattails and carefully arranged them into

a big mound. Mrs. Raccoon's home in a tall live oak had survived the storm, and she spent the day cooking. Hooter found a new nest that had belonged to another bird who had vacated it. (Owls don't care much for building their own nest.) After clearing a large space for the celebration, Mr. Bear moved his family to a bigger cypress tree cavity and set about collecting acorns to stock his new pantry.

Swampmaster Bejeaux and Tootles were oblivious
to the goings-on. Even an empty stomach could not
awaken Swampmaster Bejeaux. Arlene checked in on
him from time to time to make sure that he was resting
comfortably. She left a note tacked to a nearby cypress
tree for him to see when he finally awoke.

The day of work and preparation ended, and
the creatures were satisfied that their new homes were
adequate and preparations for the celebration were
complete. They settled in for the night.

When Swampmaster Bejeaux finally stirred the
following morning, he found that he was much improved.
He removed his cast and saw that his wound was

beginning to heal. He felt rested and revitalized. Tootles had faithfully stayed by his side to greet him when he woke and was very relieved to see him in such a good mood.

"Swampmaster Bejeaux, look at this note that someone left. What does it say?"

"Looks like we'z invited to a 'welcome home' party today. I do hope dere will be lots of food since I have a mighty hunger. But first I plan to find us a new home. Swampmaster Bejeaux spent a few hours building a new nest of sticks, leaves, and mud in a sheltered spot near the bayou. He gathered Spanish moss to make a new mattress for himself and also one for Tootles. After he finished his work, he washed his overalls and bandanna and laid them on a cypress tree branch to dry.

By lunchtime he was all spiffed up and polished-looking for the celebration. As he walked into the clearing that Mr. Bear had prepared, his friends cheered and offered him the seat-of-honor on a large tree branch.

"Welcome home, Swampmaster Bejeaux," they shouted in unison. "We are so relieved that you survived your adventure and came back home where you belong."

"I'z glad to be home, for true," Swampmaster Bejeaux admitted sincerely. "I don't deserve such a warm welcome an' such good friends. I'z been a selfish ol' gator, for true. But I'z learned mah lesson, an' I plan to be a better swamp master from now on. An' I hope you will welcome mah loyal friend an' companion, Tootles."

"He is most welcome to stay here with us," Arlene spoke. "Any friend of Swampmaster Bejeaux's is a friend of ours."

"I am grateful to hear it, and I will stay on for a while before I return to my home," Tootles replied, starting to feel a bit homesick himself.

"An' do you think it would be a good time to eat?" Swampmaster Bejeaux inquired, having eyed some of the many dishes that had been prepared.

Swampmaster Bejeaux was quickly served the delectable fish pie and cobbler which he relished with grunts of pleasure. After Swampmaster Bejeaux had savored the last bite of Mrs. Raccoon's delicious meal, his friends clamored for him to tell them about his adventures. Swampmaster Bejeaux loved being the center of attention. He began his tale at the beginning and took great care to include everything that had happened on his adventure. But as he was telling his story, he just couldn't help himself from adding a few spicy details (of the made-up variety).

"An' dat ol' loup-garou jumped right in front of mah path an' growled ferociously," Swampmaster Bejeaux stated. "But I stood mah ground, for true, an' tol' him dat he shouldn't frighten children no mo'. I made dat ol' werewolf feel so bad 'bout hisself dat he started to howl an' cry. He finally slinked off into de woods, and I'z thinkin' dat he jus' might change his mean ways."

Later on in his narrative, Swampmaster Bejeaux brought up the wood loa.

"An' jus' as dat big ol' cottonmouth snake was tellin' me 'bout de muskrat's map, I felt de air stir 'round me, an' I heard somethin' whisper in mah ear - 'You best keep on de straight an' narrow path an' git yourself back home where you belong befo' I cause you a heap of trouble.' An' dat's when I had dat very thought pop into mah own head, an' I decided right den and dere dat I was gonna stop mah travelin' an' come back to you, mah friends."

When Swampmaster Bejeaux finally finished his long-winded story, the animals were amazed and impressed by his courage and fortitude. They praised him and told him what a fine alligator they thought he was.

Swampmaster Bejeaux was quite pleased with himself and very happy to be home among loyal friends. And Swampmaster Bejeaux was true to his words. He resumed his life on Bayou Lafourche and was content to stay close to home for a while.

But whether or not that was the last of Swampmaster Bejeaux's travels remains to be seen. And whether or not the loup-garou and wood loa really exist, that is for you to decide, dear reader, because I am not quite sure myself.

Nancy Backus Roniger received a BA degree from Newcomb College of Tulane University and a MAET (Masters of Arts in English Teaching) from the University of New Orleans. She has been a teacher of grammar, writing, and literature for many years in the New Orleans area and is the author of *The Duchesses of Paducah*, a young adult novel about her childhood. She has spent her adult life soaking up the history of New Orleans and the surrounding region. She particularly enjoys all things Cajun, which inspired her book about an alligator. Nancy now lives in Madisonville, La. with her husband, Tim, and three cats. This book is dedicated to her grandchildren.

Missi

Bayou Lafourche

ayou Geneve

Swampmaster
Bejeaux's Home

nb

Swamplands

Bayou Cane